DEAD POINT

JEFF GARRISON

This is a work of fiction. Names, characters, places, and incidents either are the product of the author's imagination or are used fictitiously. Any resemblance to actual persons, living or dead, events, or locales is entirely coincidental.

First edition 2026

CHAPTER 1: THE BAR

The Christmas lights were still up.

Not because I'd forgotten. Because the members asked. Diane Kessler brought it up at the bar on a Tuesday, three days after New Year's, while I was boxing up the garland from the front entrance. She set her sauvignon blanc on the counter and said, "Leave them, Jack. The place looks better this way." And then Margaret Odem, who hasn't agreed with Diane Kessler on anything since the 2019 court resurfacing debate, said, "She's right. Leave them up." When those two women find common ground, you listen. You don't ask questions. You plug the lights back in and pour the wine.

So the lights stayed. Little warm-white LEDs strung along the rafters and around the bar posts, blinking on a timer from four in the afternoon until close. They made the club look softer. Smaller. Like someone had turned the volume down on the whole building, which, if I'm being accurate, someone had. Marcus Wells had been dead for six weeks and the club was still recalibrating. People came in quieter. They ordered simpler drinks. The couples who used to argue at Table 7 on Friday nights had stopped arguing, or stopped coming, or both. Even the sound of the paddles was different — less percussive, more careful, as if the members were hitting the ball with the awareness that noise draws attention and attention, in the post-Marcus world, was something to be managed.

I understood the impulse. After the investigation, after the arrest, after the killer's name hit the local news and then the Denver Post and then, briefly, a true crime podcast that one of my members had the poor judgment to play on the patio speakers, the club had become a place that people associated with a story. Not the story of a good facility with well-maintained courts and a bartender who remembers your drink. The story of a man who was murdered. And the members — the ones who stayed, the ones who renewed — wanted the club to feel like something other than a crime scene. Hence the lights. Hence the quieter drinks. Hence the careful paddles and the unspoken agreement that nobody mentions Marcus by name during court time, the way families don't mention the uncle who went to prison during Thanksgiving dinner. Not because they've forgotten. Because the meal is better without him at the table.

I was wiping down the bar on a Wednesday evening in late January when Navarro came in. He didn't announce himself. He never does. He just appeared on the stool at the far end — the one closest to the wall, farthest from the door — and set his phone facedown on the counter the way he always sets it facedown, screen against the wood, as if the calls he doesn't take are more important than the ones he does.

"Club soda," he said.

"Lime?"

"Sure."

I poured it. Set it on a napkin. He didn't touch it.

We'd been doing this since Christmas. Not every week — his schedule didn't allow for that — but often enough that I'd started keeping a bottle of Topo Chico in the back cooler because Navarro doesn't like the generic club soda and he's too polite to say so. He'd come in on a weeknight, usually after eight, usually alone. He'd sit at the end of the bar and drink club soda and we'd talk about nothing for twenty minutes and then he'd leave a ten on the counter for a three-dollar drink and walk out into the parking lot without saying goodbye. It was the friendship of two men who had survived the same story and didn't need to rehash it. He'd caught a killer. I'd lost thirty-two thousand dollars to a dead man's investment fund and nearly lost my club in the process. We'd both come out the other side with the specific, unglamorous relief of people who got hurt but not destroyed, and the Wednesday evening club sodas were our way of acknowledging that without having to say it out loud.

But tonight was different. Navarro was quiet in the way I'd learned to recognize — not his usual quiet, which was the comfortable silence of a man who spends his days asking questions and values the hours when he doesn't have to. This was the other quiet. The working quiet. The quiet of a man who's turning something over in his head and hasn't decided yet whether to put it on the bar.

I gave him five minutes. Wiped glasses. Restocked the limes. Let the silence do what silence does when you give it enough room, which is become uncomfortable enough that someone fills it.

"I've got a dead climber in Golden," Navarro said. He said it to the club soda, not to me. "Owner of a gym. Summit Wall, over on Ford Street. Fell on a route in Clear Creek Canyon he's done a hundred times. Piece of protection failed — a camming device. Spring-loaded thing you jam in a crack. Holds your weight if it's placed right."

"And it wasn't placed right."

"It was placed wrong in a way that looked right. Which is a very specific kind of wrong." He turned the glass. The carbonation caught the Christmas lights and threw tiny reflections across the bar top. "Coroner says the fall killed him. Gear manufacturer says the cam was functional. So either a man who's been climbing for twenty-five years forgot how to place protection on a route he could do in his sleep, or someone placed it for him."

"Sounds like an accident."

"It does." He picked up the glass. Took a sip. Set it down. "That's what bothers me."

I leaned against the back counter and crossed my arms. I knew what was coming. Not because Navarro was predictable — he wasn't — but because I'd learned, over six weeks of Wednesday evenings, that Rafael Navarro didn't bring his cases to a bartender's counter unless he wanted something the case file couldn't give him. He had forensics. He had interviews. He had the institutional machinery of the Jefferson County Sheriff's Office. What he didn't have — what he came here for — was a second pair of eyes that didn't belong to a cop.

"You want me to look at something," I said.

"I want you to visit the gym. Walk around. Talk to the wife. Talk to the staff. Tell me what you see." He looked up from the glass for the first time. "Not what happened. I can figure out what happened. What the room feels like. You're good at rooms, Jack."

"I'm good at *this* room."

"You're good at all of them. You just don't know it yet."

I didn't agree to anything right away because I've learned that agreeing to things right away is how you end up losing thirty-two thousand dollars to a man named Marcus Wells. So I finished my shift. I locked up the club. I stood in the parking lot with the Christmas lights blinking behind me in the January dark, breath visible, stars sharp, the Front Range a black wall against a blacker sky. And I thought about Owen Marsh — a man I'd never met, falling through cold air in a canyon I'd never visited, trusting a piece of metal that someone had turned into a lie.

Then I went home and looked up Summit Wall Climbing Co. on my phone. Because the bartender who reads rooms had been asked to read a new one, and the bartender who reads rooms always says yes. It's the flaw that makes him useful and the flaw that keeps getting him hurt, and after forty-seven years on the planet he has stopped pretending that the flaw and the man are different things.

CHAPTER 2: THE WALL

Summit Wall Climbing Co. occupied a converted warehouse on Ford Street in Golden, two blocks from the creek and across the street from a brewery that had a chalkboard out front advertising something called a "Hazy Mystic IPA," which told you everything you needed to know about the kind of town Golden had become. The building was industrial in the way that businesses in these mountain-adjacent communities like to be industrial — steel beams and exposed ductwork, but polished, intentional, the roughness preserved as an aesthetic choice rather than a budgetary one. Someone had spent real money making this place look like no one had spent real money on it.

I parked in the lot at ten on a Thursday morning and sat in my truck for a minute before going in. Old habit. I do the same thing before opening the club — sit in the lot, look at the building, read the outside before the inside. It's the part of the room that people forget to stage.

The lot told me three things. First, the gym was doing well: the spaces were half-full on a weekday morning, and the cars were the right mix — Subarus and Tacomas and the occasional Tesla, the fleet of a community that earns enough to have hobbies and chooses hobbies that leave dirt on the floorboards. Second, someone had placed a memorial at the base of the entrance — a framed photo of a man in a climbing harness, grinning at the camera from what looked like a ledge halfway up a red rock face, with a small pile of carabiners and chalk bags arranged around it like offerings. The photo was weatherproof. The frame was good. Someone had thought about this, which meant someone was managing the grief, which meant the grief was being performed at least partly for an audience. Third, at the far end of the lot, there was a leased Subaru Outback with a cracked windshield and a registration sticker that had expired in November. Two months past due. The car of a person who either couldn't afford the renewal or couldn't be bothered with it, and in my experience those two conditions are usually the same condition.

Inside, Summit Wall opened up into a space that made my club look like a closet. The main floor was enormous — forty-foot walls on three sides, covered in holds of every color, routes marked with tape, the walls angled and textured to simulate real rock. A bouldering section along the west wall, maybe fifteen feet high, with thick crash pads below. Ropes hanging from anchors at the top. The smell was chalk and rubber and sweat and something else, something I recognized from the club — the specific humidity of a space where people come to exert themselves in the company of other people who are exerting themselves, the communal body heat of effort.

There were maybe twenty people climbing. A woman on a top rope near the entrance, moving with the mechanical precision of someone working a route she'd done before. Two men on the bouldering wall, alternating attempts on a problem that involved an overhang and a lot of grunting. A group of four in the back, near what looked like a training area, doing pull-ups on a hangboard — a strip of wood with different-sized holds, designed to build the finger strength that climbing requires and that no other sport on earth prepares you for.

I stood at the front counter and took it in.

What I saw was a terrarium. The same thing I'd seen when I first stood behind the bar at my club and watched the members perform their rituals — the warm-ups, the greetings, the casual cruelties disguised as banter. A sealed ecosystem with its own hierarchy, its own language, its own unspoken rules about who belongs and who is tolerated and who is invisible. The climbing gym was younger and leaner and more physical than the pickleball club, and the trust dynamics were different — in climbing, you literally put your life in another person's hands every time you tie in, which builds a kind of intimacy that no amount of pickleball partnership can replicate. But the social mechanics were identical. Hierarchies. Performances. The theater of belonging. Different stage, same play.

Keira Marsh found me before I found her. She came out of a glass-walled office behind the front desk — operations, from the look of it, spreadsheets visible on a monitor — and walked toward me with the measured pace of a woman who has decided in advance how this interaction will go. Late thirties. Dark hair pulled back. Fit in the understated way of someone who exercises as maintenance rather than performance. She was wearing a Summit Wall staff shirt and no jewelry except a thin gold chain with a pendant I couldn't identify from across the counter.

"You must be the friend of Detective Navarro's," she said. Not a question.

"Jack Brennan. I appreciate you making time."

"Owen would have wanted the gym to cooperate fully." She said it evenly, with the kind of composure that could have been rehearsal or could have been shock. "Owen's energy is still in this space. I feel him on the walls. On the routes he set. In the chalk on the holds." She touched the counter with her fingertips, lightly, as if receiving a signal. "He's not gone. He's just climbing somewhere we can't follow."

I've tended bar for twelve years. I've watched hundreds of people grieve at my counter — real grief, the ugly kind, the kind that forgets to close its mouth and orders the wrong drink and leaves without paying. What Keira Marsh was doing at the front desk of her dead husband's gym wasn't obviously that. But it wasn't obviously a performance, either. It was something in between — the dissociated calm of a woman who might be three steps behind her own tragedy and hadn't yet noticed the gap, or the careful calm of a woman who was exactly where she meant to be. I couldn't tell yet. Not being able to tell is the tell I pay attention to.

I nodded. Said the right things. Asked her about the gym, about Owen's routines, about the morning of the climb. She answered each question cleanly — too cleanly, or maybe just cleanly enough. I filed it. Didn't push. A woman can sound scripted because she's performing and she can sound scripted because she's told the same story to six different cops in the last two weeks, and from the outside those two conditions look identical.

Then I went to find the bouldering wall.

Nate Calloway was twenty-three and looked it — the kind of lean that comes from climbing every day and eating when you remember to. He was soloing a V7 on the overhang, no rope, no pad spotter, just a man and a wall and the specific aggression of someone using his body to solve a problem that his mind can't touch. His forearms were veined. His chalk bag left white prints on every hold. He moved with a fluidity that I recognized as talent — not learned technique but the innate spatial intelligence of a person whose body understands geometry the way a musician's hands understand intervals.

He was also wrecked. Red eyes. Hands that shook when he chalked up between attempts. The physical signature of a man who hasn't slept in days, or who has slept but not well, which is a different and worse condition. I've seen it at the bar — the members who come in after a divorce, after a diagnosis, after the thing that rearranges the furniture in your chest. They order their regular drink and their hands tremble and they don't notice because the trembling has become the baseline. The anxiety didn't just follow him; it curdled in the air around him. But the trembling wasn't the tell. The tell was what the trembling did when he touched the wall — it stopped. The second his fingers found the holds, his hands went steady as a surgeon's. The kid had shaking hands everywhere except on climbing gear, and that is a very specific kind of shaking.

Nate came off the wall and saw me watching. He didn't introduce himself. He pulled a water bottle from his bag — a dented Nalgene with stickers peeling off the sides — and drank half of it without stopping.

"Jack," I said. "Friend of Navarro's."

"Yeah." He wiped his mouth with the back of his hand. "Keira said you were coming."

"How are you doing?"

He looked at me. And here's the thing I couldn't name yet, the thing I'd come to find without knowing it: underneath the grief, underneath the red eyes and the shaking hands and the aggressive soloing, there was something else. Not guilt, exactly. Something more like *waiting*. The quiet, coiled patience of a man who is in a room he doesn't plan to stay in, passing through on his way to somewhere he believes is better. I'd seen it before — on Marcus Wells, in the weeks before Vertex collapsed, the serenity of a man who knew the game was almost over and had already calculated which door he was walking out of.

"I'm managing," Nate said. He said it to the water bottle.

"Owen was a good guy. Everyone says so."

"Owen was the best person I've ever known." And this was real — the voice cracked, the eyes filled, the grief surfaced for a half-second before something pulled it back under, the way a fish breaks the surface and then disappears. "He gave me everything. This job. This community. He trusted me." He paused. "He trusted everyone. That was his gift."

"Sounds like it was also his problem."

Nate looked at me then — a quick, sharp look, the first unscripted moment since I'd walked in — and I saw something move behind his eyes that he didn't want me to see. Then it was gone.

"I should get back to setting," he said. "Route resets are on Thursdays. Owen's schedule. I'm keeping it."

He turned and walked toward the far wall, chalk bag swinging, and I stood in the bouldering area of a dead man's gym and thought about what I'd seen. The composed widow with her careful vocabulary. The wrecked twenty-three-year-old with the expert hands and the sharp look and the car in the lot with the expired tags. The memorial at the entrance with the weatherproof frame.

Two reads. One composed to the point of glass. One wrecked to the point of splintering. And underneath both of them, a dead man who trusted everyone and fell through cold air in a canyon because a piece of metal was placed the specific kind of wrong that looks right — the specific kind of wrong that takes expertise to engineer. Only one of the two people I'd just talked to had that expertise, and it wasn't the woman behind the front desk. That was a thought I wasn't ready to build a case around, but I wasn't ready to set it down, either.

I texted Navarro from the parking lot: *Gym's a terrarium. Come see me Wednesday.*

Then I drove home on I-70 with the mountains in my mirrors and the feeling — familiar now, unwelcome — that

I'd just walked into another room I wasn't going to be able to walk out of.

CHAPTER 3: THE PARTNER

Sloane Decker was already at the taproom on Washington Avenue when I got there. She'd picked a table near the window, which told me something about her before she said a word: she wanted to see the street. She wanted to see who was coming. She was a woman who preferred her back to the wall and her eyes on the door, and I liked her immediately because that's exactly how I arrange myself behind my bar.

She was early forties, short brown hair, no makeup, the kind of face that broadcasting coaches would call "strong" when they mean a woman who doesn't look like she's trying to look like anything. She was drinking a porter — not a hazy IPA, not a sour, not one of the fourteen experimental offerings that Golden's brewery scene produces with the relentless optimism of a town that believes every problem can be solved with hops. A porter. A beer that tastes like what it is. Another thing to like.

"Jack," she said, when I sat down. "You're the bartender."

"I'm the bartender."

"Navarro said you'd be coming around. He said you're 'observant.'" She put air quotes around it. "Which is cop for 'useful but not one of us.'"

"That's about right."

She studied me for a moment the way I imagine she studies a climbing route — reading the holds, calculating the sequence, deciding whether the risk is worth the energy. Then she took a drink of her porter and set it down and said, "Owen was the best man I've ever known, and I need you to understand that before I tell you anything else, because what I'm going to tell you is going to sound like I'm criticizing him and I'm not. I'm describing him. There's a difference."

"I understand the difference."

"Good. Because most people don't."

She told me about Owen Marsh. Not the memorial version — the weatherproof photo at the entrance, the chalked-up holds, the social media tributes that had been accumulating on Summit Wall's Instagram like flowers on a roadside cross. She told me the version that the people closest to him knew, the version that only comes out at a table near the window in a taproom on a Thursday afternoon, between a woman who lost her climbing partner and a bartender who was asked to listen.

Owen was kind. That was the foundation, the load-bearing wall. Kind in the specific, uncomplicated way that certain men are kind — without agenda, without performance, without needing credit for it. He remembered birthdays. He belayed beginners on their first climb with the patience of a man who understood that the first time someone trusts a rope is a holy moment whether they know it or not. He comped memberships for kids who couldn't afford them and didn't put their names on a board or write it off as marketing. He was the kind of gym owner who mopped his own floors at midnight because the cleaning crew canceled and the morning crew deserved a clean facility.

"He was also completely, catastrophically blind to the people around him," Sloane said. She said it without anger. With the flat precision of a woman who has been thinking about this for weeks and has arrived at an assessment she doesn't enjoy but won't soften. "Not stupid. Never stupid. Blind. Owen looked at the people he loved and saw the people he wanted them to be, and the distance between those two things — the version he saw and the version that existed — that distance was where all the damage happened."

"The distance sounds familiar."

"I bet it does."

She told me about Keira's transformation. It started about two years before Owen died — the Pilates studio, Inner Mountain, three mornings a week. That was fine. Normal. A woman in her late thirties taking reformer classes in Golden, Colorado, was about as remarkable as a man in his forties joining a pickleball club. It was the on-ramp to a community, and the community was the point, and if the community had a slightly spiritual tilt — breathwork workshops, crystal bowls in the lobby, a vocabulary that favored "intention" and "alignment" over "plan" and "goal" — well, this was the Front Range, and you couldn't throw a yoga block without hitting someone who'd replaced their therapist with a sound bath.

But then the vocabulary changed. Keira started talking about energy in a way that had weight to it, specificity, the language of a person who had crossed the line from interest to belief. She mentioned "soul contracts." She mentioned "karmic cycles." She mentioned, once, at a gym barbecue, that she and Owen had been "together in past lives" and that their relationship in this one was "part of a larger spiritual curriculum," and Sloane had excused herself to get another beer because there is no polite response to being told that your friend's marriage is homework assigned by the universe.

"And then she found Nate," Sloane said.

"Or Nate found her."

"Does it matter?" She turned her glass. "She started coming to the gym different. Not better, not worse — *focused*. Like she'd found the thing she'd been looking for at Inner Mountain and the thing turned out to be a twenty-three-year-old with a yoga mat and a jawline. She told Owen he had to hire this guy. Great climber. Great instructor. Great *energy*." The air quotes again. "And Owen did, because Owen did whatever Keira asked, because Owen loved his wife the way he loved his routes — completely, confidently, without looking down."

She drank. Set the glass down. Ran her thumb along the condensation.

"I told him. Once." Her voice dropped, not to a whisper but to the specific register of a person revisiting a conversation they wish they'd handled differently. "I said, 'Owen, your wife looks at Nate like he's a religion.' He laughed. Not a dismissive laugh — a genuine one, the laugh of a man who couldn't imagine the sentence being true because imagining it would require imagining that his wife was capable of something he wasn't capable of imagining. He said, 'Keira's into the spiritual stuff. She looks at everyone like that.' And I let it go."

"Because what do you say."

"Because what do you say. How do you tell a good man that his wife's faith is aimed at another man? He wouldn't have heard it. Good men never hear it. They hear the version that lets them keep being good, because the alternative — the version where goodness isn't enough, where trusting people isn't a virtue but a vulnerability — that version rewrites everything they believe about themselves, and good men would rather fall off a mountain than do that."

She stopped. Looked out the window at Washington Avenue, at the winter afternoon, at the steady traffic of a mountain town going about its business.

"They never touched," she said. "Not even after Crestone. Keira and Nate. I watched them for eighteen months. Eighteen months of existing in the same building every day, orbiting each other with a gravity I could feel from across the gym. The way they stood near each other — not too close, never too close, but in each other's *field,* like two magnets held just far enough apart that you couldn't call it contact but close enough that everything between them was charged. They never held hands. Never hugged longer than a colleague would hug. Never left together, arrived together, none of it. But."

"But."

"But I've been climbing for twenty years, Jack. I know what trust looks like on a rope. I know what it looks like when two people are connected by a line they can't see but can feel. Keira and Nate were on belay with each other every second of every day, and Owen was free-soloing three feet away and didn't even know there was a route."

She finished her porter. Didn't order another. She looked at me with the clear, undecorated expression of a woman who has said everything she came to say and is waiting to find out if the man she said it to was worth the trip.

"Owen Marsh was the best man I've ever known," she said again. "And the thing about the best men is that they make it easy. They make it so easy to love them that you forget there are people in the world who experience ease as an opportunity. Who see a man with no defenses and think, 'Good. One less thing to get through.'"

She stood up. Pulled on her jacket. Paused.

"Find out what happened on that wall, Jack. Owen deserves the real version. Not the weatherproof one."

She left. I sat at the table near the window and watched her walk down Washington Avenue toward Clear Creek, hands in her pockets, head down, the posture of a woman carrying a weight that no one else can see because the weight is shaped like a man who trusted everyone, and everyone included whichever of them had taken the trust and made it into a rope.

I ordered a porter. Drank it slowly. Thought about magnets and gravity and the space between people who never touch, and how the space between people who never touch can be more dangerous than the contact, because contact has evidence and distance has deniability and deniability, in my experience, is where murder lives.

CHAPTER 4: THE FLAME

Inner Mountain Studio was in a strip mall on South Golden Road, between a pet grooming place and a shop that sold handmade candles with names like “Solstice” and “Grounding Ritual.” The strip mall itself was clean, well-maintained, the parking lot freshly sealed — the kind of commercial space that in most towns would house a dry cleaner and a Subway franchise but in Golden, Colorado, housed a Pilates-yoga fusion studio and a candle shop that probably grossed more than both. I’ve seen it from behind the bar — members who spend more on recovery than they spend on the sport, women who do reformer Pilates at seven, hot yoga at noon, and infrared sauna at five, and then come to my club at seven-thirty to play recreational pickleball with the serene exhaustion of people who have spent the entire day maintaining a body they’ll never be satisfied with. It’s an industry built on the promise that if you bend enough, stretch enough, breathe enough, you’ll arrive at a version of yourself that doesn’t need any of it. Nobody arrives. Everyone renews.

I walked in at two in the afternoon. The studio was in its quiet hours — the morning reformer rush was over and the evening crowd hadn't arrived yet. The lobby was exactly what I expected: natural wood, a shoe rack, a small retail display of yoga mats and blocks and the kind of water bottles that cost forty dollars because they're made from "responsibly sourced bamboo." There was a bowl of crystals on the front desk — amethyst, rose quartz, the usual suspects — arranged next to a stack of business cards for a breathwork practitioner named Sage who specialized in "somatic release and energetic alignment." Behind the desk, through a glass partition, I could see a row of Pilates reformers — sleek, low machines that looked like medieval torture devices designed by someone with a Scandinavian furniture catalog — and beyond them, a larger room with yoga mats arranged in a circle. The smell was lavender and cedar and clean sweat. The music was the kind of ambient sound that's designed to make you feel spiritual but mostly makes you feel like you're on hold with a very expensive therapist.

Ray Calloway came out of a back office when the front desk girl told him someone was asking about Keira Marsh. He was late fifties, built like a man who'd been doing his own product for three decades — lean, flexible, the kind of posture that makes chiropractors jealous. He had close-cropped gray hair and reading glasses pushed up on his forehead and the expression of a man who had been expecting someone like me and wishing he hadn't been right.

"You're the one working with the detective," he said. Not unfriendly. Careful.

Ray looked at me for a long moment, the way a man looks at a contractor he didn't hire, trying to decide if the work is worth the disruption. Then he nodded once — a resigned nod, the nod of a man who is going to cooperate not because he wants to but because the alternative is carrying what he's carrying alone, and the weight has gotten heavy enough that a stranger's ears are better than no ears at all.

"Come on," he said. "I'll show you the space."

He walked me through Inner Mountain the way I walk visitors through my club — not with pride exactly, but with the proprietary attention of a man who built something with his hands and maintains it with his habits. The reformer room first: twelve machines, all occupied during peak hours, mostly women in their thirties and forties, some men, a mix of serious athletes and recreational benders. The yoga room: heated, with a capacity of thirty, used for everything from vinyasa to yin to the breathwork workshops that happened on Saturday mornings and drew a specific clientele that Ray described with the diplomatic precision of a man who has learned to love his customers without endorsing their beliefs.

"Most of my people are here for the workout," he said. "Some of them are here for the community. And a few of them are here because they're looking for something they can't name and they think flexibility is a metaphor."

"Is it?"

"It's flexibility. You get better at touching your toes. What you do with the feelings that come up when you touch your toes — that's between you and your nervous system."

He showed me the lobby where people gathered after classes — the social hub, the informal community space, the place where friendships formed and deepened and, occasionally, curdled into something more intense. He pointed out the retail display, the crystal bowl, the breathwork cards. He said the studio had been open for fifteen years, that he'd built it from a single room in this same strip mall, that the expansion into reformer Pilates four years ago had doubled his revenue and tripled his headaches because the Pilates crowd expected a level of facility maintenance that the yoga crowd considered spiritually irrelevant.

Then he stopped near the window, where the afternoon light came through the glass and lit up the dust in the air, and his posture changed. Shifted from tour guide to something heavier.

"Keira was a member for about two years," he said. "Three mornings a week. Committed. Showed up, did the work, stayed for the lobby chats. Normal. Healthy. One of the good ones." He paused. "Then she started doing the Saturday breathwork. And the breathwork — look, I offer it because there's demand. Some people genuinely benefit. It regulates the nervous system, there's research. But some people use breathwork the way some people use alcohol. Not for the thing itself but for the permission it gives them to feel things they won't let themselves feel on a Tuesday afternoon in their own kitchen."

"I know the type. I pour for them."

"Then you know. Keira went deep. The Saturday workshops led to the weekday community, the community led to the online forums, the forums led to —" He stopped.

Rubbed the back of his neck. “But one day she was talking about breathwork and nervous system regulation and the next day she was talking about soul contracts and karmic clearings and I thought, okay, she’s found a framework. People find frameworks. It’s not my job to edit their metaphysics.”

“But then Nate.”

Ray went quiet. The specific quiet of a man arriving at the part of the story he’s been dreading.

“I don’t know why I am telling you all of this” he said. “Nate’s my sister’s kid. Linda’s boy. He’s been around this studio since he was fifteen — helped me set up reformers, mopped floors, the whole bit. Smart kid. Good climber. No direction.” He looked at the reformer room through the glass. “I gave him the Thursday evening class because he needed the money and he’s good at leading a room. Yoga-for-climbers mobility. It’s a niche class — draws a mix, mostly people who climb and want to stay flexible, some people who want to try climbing and think yoga is the on-ramp. The Thursday class was Nate’s. I didn’t think about it. I gave my twenty-three-year-old nephew a room full of people looking for connection and a platform to connect from, and I told myself I was helping him build a career.”

He paused. Looked at the crystals on the front desk.

"Keira started staying after the Thursday class. Nate would finish leading the session and she'd be there in the lobby, and they'd talk. Not flirting — I'd have noticed flirting. This was different. Deeper. They talked the way people talk when they've discovered a shared language that nobody else speaks. The twin flame vocabulary — I heard pieces of it. 'Recognition.' 'Mirror soul.' 'The Runner and the Chaser.' They had a whole taxonomy for what was happening between them, and the taxonomy made it feel academic instead of what it was."

"Which was what?"

"A thirty-eight-year-old married woman and my twenty-three-year-old nephew building something neither of them had the self-awareness to call by its right name." He said it flat. No drama. The delivery of a man who has rehearsed this sentence enough times that it's lost its heat but not its weight. "And I watched it. For months. I watched it build in my lobby, after my classes, in my studio. And I told myself it wasn't my business because I sell reformer sessions and hot yoga and what people do with the feelings afterward is between them and their therapist." He paused. "Or their divorce attorney."

Another pause. Longer this time.

"I gave him the class, Jack. I gave my sister's kid a class full of women in their thirties and forties who are looking for something they can't name. And then I acted surprised when he found one."

I thanked Ray. He walked me to the door. At the threshold, he stopped.

"Is Nate going to be okay?" he asked. And the way he asked it — quietly, from the side of his mouth, the way a man asks a question he already knows the answer to — told me that Ray Calloway understood more than he'd said. That the question wasn't really about whether Nate was going to be okay. It was about whether the thing that Ray had given Nate — the class, the platform, the room — had contributed to the thing that happened to Owen. And the answer was yes, the same way the answer is always yes when someone builds a stage and doesn't ask what's going to be performed on it.

"I don't know," I said. Because I didn't. And because lying to a man who is already lying to himself doesn't help either of you.

I went home. Sat in my truck in my own parking lot and opened my phone and typed "twin flame" into the search bar and spent the next three hours falling down a hole that made me want to pour bleach into my eyes.

The forums were the worst part. Hundreds of people — thousands — all reinforcing each other's delusions with the specific enthusiasm of a community that has confused consensus with truth. "Trust the journey." "Your karmic partner is the lesson; your twin flame is the reward." It was the same language Marcus Wells used on his investors, repackaged with crystals and breathwork: believe in something hard enough and the believing makes it real. Except it doesn't. Believing in a thing doesn't make it real. It makes you committed. And commitment without reality is just a more expensive word for obsession.

I found Keira's posts on a forum called TheTwinFlameJourney.com, posted under a handle that was transparently her — same age, same location, same story details. Eighteen months of entries. Eighteen months of documenting "the Recognition" and "the Runner/Chaser dynamic" and "the karmic clearing that must occur before union." She wrote about Owen without naming him — "my 3D partner," she called him, "my karmic contract" — with the clinical detachment of a woman who had already, in the architecture of her belief system, filed him under "temporary." She wrote about Nate — "my DM," her Divine Masculine — with a reverence that made my skin crawl, not because it was sexual but because it was *certain*. There was no doubt in these posts. No questioning. No moment where she stepped outside the framework and asked herself whether the framework might be the problem. She was inside it the way a fish is inside water — completely, invisibly, without any awareness that there was an outside.

And then I found Nate's posts. Different forum. Different handle. Same mythology. His posts were about "the Divine Feminine" who had appeared in his life and "the karmic bonds" preventing their union and "the energetic clearing that the universe will perform when the time is right." He wasn't a passive recipient of Keira's delusion. He was an active co-author. They'd been writing the same story from two keyboards, in two forums, for eighteen months, and the story had a protagonist (their union), and a villain (Owen), and a resolution (the universe would remove the obstacle), and neither of them had the honesty or the courage to write the ending in plain language, which is: we want him gone, and we're building a mythology to make wanting it feel like destiny instead of desire.

I closed my phone. Sat in the dark parking lot. The Christmas lights were blinking behind me through the club windows.

Twin flames. The theory is that your soul was split in two before you were born, and the other half is walking around somewhere, and when you find them, you feel a "recognition" that transcends ordinary attraction. It's the romantic version of finding your car keys in the last place you look — retrospectively obvious, spiritually meaningless, and a convenient explanation for why you're willing to blow up your life for a person you've known for six months.

I went inside. Locked up. Poured a bourbon I didn't need and drank it standing at my bar in the empty club, and thought about the distance between belief and delusion and how, from the inside, there is no distance at all.

CHAPTER 5: THE ROUTE

Navarro picked me up on a Saturday morning in an unmarked Jeep Cherokee that smelled like coffee and old case files. He drove west on US-6 toward Clear Creek Canyon with the unhurried precision of a man who has driven this road enough times to stop seeing the scenery, which was a shame because the scenery was the kind of thing that postcards were invented for — red and gray rock walls rising from the creek bed, the water low and dark in January, the road winding between the walls like a suture through a wound.

"The route is called Coney Island," Navarro said. He was wearing his weekend clothes — jeans, a fleece, hiking boots — but his posture was still cop posture, the permanent alertness of a man whose profession requires him to treat every environment as a potential crime scene. "Five-ten-a. Traditional. It's about eighty feet, three pitches, on the south-facing wall of the canyon. Moderate route. The kind of thing experienced climbers use as a warm-up."

"And Owen was experienced."

"Owen Marsh was one of the most experienced trad climbers in the Front Range. He'd been climbing since he was nineteen. The man wrote a blog post — I read it — about the importance of inspecting every piece of gear before every climb, titled 'Trust Your Gear, Verify Your Gear.'" Navarro shook his head. "The irony is not lost on the investigation."

He pulled off the road at a turnout near a metal bridge and we walked down a trail that followed the creek to the base of the wall. The rock was beautiful in the way that Colorado rock is beautiful — not dramatic like Yosemite, not otherworldly like Utah, but solid and textured and old, the kind of rock that looks like it was designed by someone who valued function over spectacle. The face where Owen fell was about thirty feet from the trail, a clean vertical wall with a crack system running up the center like a seam in a piece of fabric.

"Second pitch," Navarro said, pointing up. "About forty feet up. He was leading — that means he's climbing first, placing protection as he goes, clipping the rope through the protection so that if he falls, the protection catches him.

The last piece of protection he placed before the fall was a number two Black Diamond Camalot."

"Explain it to me like I serve drinks for a living."

Navarro reached into his pack and pulled out a piece of climbing gear. It looked like a mechanical spider — four curved metal lobes arranged around a central axle, connected to a stem with a trigger.

"You squeeze this, slide it into a crack, and when you release the trigger, the lobes expand and grip the rock. Spring-loaded. The friction holds it in place. If you place it correctly — lobes evenly seated, stem pulling in the direction of a potential fall, crack parallel-sided — this thing holds thousands of pounds. You could hang a truck from it."

"And if you place it wrong?"

"If you invert it — lobes facing the wrong direction — or place it in a crack that's flared or too shallow, it looks secure. It holds body weight on a static hang. But when you fall — when there's a dynamic load, a sudden downward force — the cam rotates out of the crack. Pops like a champagne cork." He mimed it with his hand. "The rope goes slack. And you fall to whatever's below you."

“Which in this case was.”

“Forty feet of air and then a ledge.”

We stood at the base of the wall and looked up. The crack system was clean, straight, the kind of feature that even I — a man whose primary physical activity is reaching for top-shelf bottles — could identify as a logical place to put a piece of protection. The route was not dramatic. Not intimidating. It was the climbing equivalent of a road you drive every day — so familiar that you stop thinking about it, which is exactly when the road kills you.

“Owen placed three pieces of protection on the second pitch,” Navarro said. “The first two were bomber — his word, from the blog. Perfectly placed, deeply seated, textbook. The third — the one he fell on — was inverted. Lobes facing up instead of down. Stem angled wrong. In a crack that was slightly flared, which compounds the error because a flared crack gives the cam nothing to grip when it’s under load.”

“So either Owen forgot everything he knew about protection placement on the third piece of a route he’d climbed a hundred times — ”

“Or someone swapped the piece after he placed it. Or, more likely, someone swapped the piece before he climbed.” Navarro put the cam back in his pack. “Owen’s gear — his personal rack — was in his car at the trailhead. Keira drove him that morning. She’d never done that before. Owen always drove himself. Always. His climbing partner, Sloane Decker, told me he was ‘ritualistic’ about his pre-climb routine. Same car, same parking spot when he could get it, same gear check in the lot before walking to the wall.”

“But that morning Keira drove.”

“That morning Keira drove. She said Owen’s truck was making a noise and she offered to drop him off. Owen’s truck was checked by a mechanic three days after his death. No noise. No issue. The truck was fine.”

I looked up at the wall again. Forty feet. A fall you’d have time to understand, time to feel the air and the speed and the specific, terrible knowledge that the thing you trusted has failed and the ground is coming and there is nothing between you and it except the seconds it takes to arrive.

“Nate inspected Owen’s gear that morning,” Navarro said. “At the gym, before Owen left. Standard practice —

the head route-setter checks gear for the owner, the way a co-pilot checks instruments for the captain. Nate signed off. Said everything looked good."

"But the gear Owen carried up the wall wasn't the gear Nate checked."

"The gear Owen carried up the wall included at least one piece — the number two Camalot — that had been modified. Not tampered with mechanically. You can't tell from looking at it. It was placed in the rack in a way that, when Owen pulled it and slotted it into the crack on autopilot — the way you do on a route you've done a hundred times, muscle memory, not thinking — he would place it inverted. The orientation was wrong in the rack. The lobes were pre-positioned so that Owen's natural placement motion would seat them backward."

"That's not an accident."

"That is the opposite of an accident. That is someone who understands climbing protection at an expert level engineering a failure that looks like human error. That is someone who knows how Owen Marsh places a number two cam on the second pitch of Coney Island and reverse-engineered the placement to guarantee a pop under dynamic load. That is also, Jack, a very short list of people."

I thought about Nate Calloway. Twenty-three. Head route-setter. The man who understood every hold on every wall in Summit Wall, who set problems for competition climbers, who taught beginners how to place their first piece of protection. The man with the talent and the knowledge and the shaking hands and the expired registration sticker and the mythology that told him the universe was clearing the path. On the short list of people who could reverse-engineer Owen Marsh's muscle memory, Nate was the whole list.

"Who had access to Owen's gear before the climb?"

"Nate had access for eleven hours. The rack lived on a peg in the back office overnight. Nate closed up Tuesday. Nate opened Wednesday. Nate did the pre-climb inspection and signed the log and handed the bag to Owen personally." Navarro drummed his fingers once on the rock at the base of the wall. "Eleven hours alone with a rack, a number two Camalot, and the muscle memory of the man he was going to hand it to. That's not a window. That's a workshop."

"And Keira?"

Navarro looked at me. The cop look. The look that says: *I'm not ready to answer that yet.*

"Keira drove him that morning," Navarro said finally. "Which is its own anomaly. Owen always drove himself. Sloane called him ritualistic about it. Keira stayed in the car while Owen loaded his pack at the tailgate. Sixty seconds. Maybe ninety. The time it takes to kiss your husband goodbye and hand him a water bottle. Not enough time to reverse-engineer an expert placement on a piece you've never touched. Enough time to confirm something was already in the rack exactly where it was supposed to be."

"So Nate built the trap and Keira walked it to the door."

"That's one theory. There are others. Maybe Nate built the trap and walked it to the door himself and Keira drove the car because the truck had a problem that wasn't a problem. Maybe Keira watched enough YouTube to place an inverted cam without ever touching a rock. My prosecutor doesn't get to pick the clean theory, Jack. She gets to pick the one the evidence supports. Right now the evidence supports the kid in the back office with the pegboard."

I called Sloane from the parking lot. Sent her the photos Navarro had cleared me to share — the cam, the crack, the angle of placement. She didn't answer with words. She made a sound, low and involuntary, the sound of a person seeing something they've been afraid to see.

"That cam is upside down," she said. Her voice was steady but her breathing wasn't. "The lobes are facing the wrong way. Owen would never place a cam like that. He *taught* me how to place cams. He taught half the gym how to place cams." A pause. "Someone put that in his rack backward. Someone who knew exactly how Owen reaches for a number two and exactly how he seats it in a parallel crack. Someone who's watched him do it enough times to reverse the motion."

The line went quiet except for her breathing, and the breathing was the breathing of a woman who has just heard her own suspicion confirmed by evidence and is learning that confirmation doesn't feel like relief. It feels like the floor opening.

The canyon was in shadow now — the kind of late-afternoon shadow that comes down fast in winter — and the creek was running its low cold music under the ice at the edges, and I had just sent her the three photos Navarro had cleared me to send.

She made the sound, and then the sound resolved into a sentence.

“Where are you?”

“The canyon.”

“Come here. Bring your friend. I've been holding something since September and I think I've been waiting to know what it was worth.”

I looked at Navarro. He was leaning against the Ford, arms folded, watching me with the quiet patience of a man who has already clocked both ends of the phone call and is waiting to see which one wins. I didn't have to repeat it. He nodded once and got in.

Sloane's house was on a side street in north Golden, a craftsman with a porch that leaned slightly to the east and a rack of climbing shoes by the door — seven pairs, arranged by stiffness — and a dog of unspecified parentage asleep on a Pendleton blanket in front of a wood stove. The house smelled like coffee and chalk and the particular cold-air cleanness of a climber's laundry that has been drying on a rack all afternoon. She didn't drink. She made us coffee instead, and she made it the way climbers make everything, which is with more care than the situation requires.

“I should have told you both,” she said, “the first time you sat on that couch. I wasn't sure what I had. I'm sure now.”

She set her mug down. Her hands were steady. I have learned over twelve years behind a bar that the people whose hands shake when they're about to tell the truth are the amateurs. The people whose hands go still are the ones about to say something they've rehearsed for months inside their own head, waiting for someone to ask.

“In September,” she said, “Keira and Nate went on a retreat together. Five-day intensive in Crestone. Place is called Two Flames Rising. Markets itself as a healing container for — and this is their language, not mine — spiritual partners on a shared awakening arc. Keira paid the deposit on her card in June. I know because Owen made a joke about it over beers — *my wife's dropping nine hundred dollars to breathe with a stranger*. He thought it was funny. He thought it was Keira being Keira.”

Navarro wasn't writing yet. He was listening in the specific way he listens when he doesn't want the person to hear a pen.

“I was in the San Luis Valley the same week,” Sloane said. “I had a project on the Crestone Needle approach — a splitter finger crack I'd been thinking about for two seasons. Staying at the hostel in town. Day four of their retreat, day three of mine. I walked past the gate of the center at six-thirty in the morning on my way to the trailhead, and they were coming down the path toward the main road. Keira in front. Nate behind. They weren't touching. They weren't saying anything. But the space between them had been *claimed* — that's the word, claimed — in the way that two people stand near each other when the distance between their bodies is no longer a neutral distance, when the air between them is a room they've been sharing. I've been climbing with men for fifteen years. I know the difference between a partner and a partner."

"That's not something you'd take to a D.A.," Navarro said.

"No. It's something I'd take to a friend. And I didn't. That's what I'm here to say."

She told us the rest in a clean sequence, the way climbers coil a rope. A text she saw on Keira's phone in the gym lobby in October — the phone screen-up on a bench, a message from Nate that read *the container is still holding* with three heart emojis, gone by the time Keira came back from the restroom. A moonstone pendant Keira started wearing at Thanksgiving and wouldn't explain — Sloane finally asked and Keira said *it's from the retreat, it's part of my alchemical work,* and Sloane, knowing the retreat had a gift shop and knowing Keira had not bought herself jewelry in eight years, had done the math. An Instagram story Nate posted and deleted within twenty minutes in early December — a mirror selfie in what looked like the Summit Wall back office, a hand visible at the small of his back, and on the wrist of the hand a slim silver watch Sloane had seen Keira wear on every belay session for the last four years.

"And Owen," she said, and for the first time the steadiness in her hands broke, not to a tremor but to a stillness that was worse than a tremor. "Owen said something to me in October that I'll repeat exactly because I've said it to myself enough times to get it right. We were at the Buffalo Rose. He had a beer. I had a soda. He said *Keira's got her thing, I've got the gym, this is what a grown-up marriage looks like, we don't have to be fused.* He said it warmly. Like a man who was proud of the arrangement. He thought he was describing maturity. He was describing the window she was going to climb out of."

She was quiet for a moment.

"He'd lost his dad in July. Did either of you know that? He'd lost his dad in July, the lease on the gym was in renegotiation, he was leading five-eleven every weekend because that was how he grieved, and his wife was on a five-day retreat in Crestone with a twenty-three-year-old route setter whose hands only stopped shaking when they were on a hold. And Owen thought it was sweet. He thought it was Keira *helping* Nate. That was how Owen loved people. He assumed the best of them and then rearranged the evidence until the best was what he saw. If I had told him what I saw at the gate that morning in Crestone, he would have looked me in the face and said *Sloane, you're wrong about my wife.* He would have said it with the same certainty he used to place a cam. And he would have been wrong. And the wrongness wouldn't have saved him, because the wrongness was the thing Keira was counting on."

Navarro was writing now. He had stopped pretending not to.

"Dates," he said.

"First week of September. Two Flames Rising, Crestone. Keira's card — ending in something, I can't swear to the digits. Registered in Keira's name with Nate listed as her spiritual partner. I called the center three months ago, after the Instagram story — said I was thinking of registering my brother and me for the spring session and asked whether they could confirm a past alumni pair by way of reference. They gave it up like a hotel concierge."

Navarro looked at her for a long moment. The cop look. The look that is also, sometimes, the other look.

"You would have made a hell of a detective."

"I would have made a terrible detective. I spent four months not telling the one person who needed to know."

We drove back toward Golden in the gathering dark. Navarro didn't say anything for the first ten minutes. Neither did I. Somewhere past the last light of the canyon he cleared his throat.

"Crestone's the pivot. Before Crestone, two people in a gym. After Crestone, two people with a covenant. And Owen didn't see either version. Owen saw the version he married."

I thought about that for the rest of the drive. I thought about it while the truck climbed out of the canyon and the plain opened up and the lights of Golden came on one at a time like a slow constellation. The fall, I realized, had not been inevitable from the wedding. The fall had been inevitable from the first week of September, from a gate in Crestone at six-thirty in the morning, from a photograph that existed only in Sloane's memory and had been waiting four months for someone to ask her what she saw.

CHAPTER 6: THE CLEARING

I went back to Summit Wall on a Tuesday evening, after closing time. Navarro had told Keira I'd be coming. She'd left the side door unlocked and the lights on and nothing else — no greeting, no chaperone, no instructions. Just an open door and a lit gym and, somewhere inside it, the man I'd come to talk to.

Nate was on the wall. Thirty feet up, free-soloing a route on the overhang that even I — a man whose understanding of climbing begins and ends with the metaphorical kind — could recognize as reckless. No rope. No harness. No protection. Just his hands and his shoes and the chalk on his fingertips and the crash pad below, which at thirty feet would do roughly the same amount of good as a napkin under a falling piano. He was climbing fast, punching through moves with the controlled violence of a man who is using his body to solve something that his mind refuses to touch.

I stood at the base of the wall and watched him climb. The gym was empty. The lights hummed. The crash pad was scuffed and chalked and dented in the places where bodies had landed — some gracefully, some not. Above me, Nate moved across the overhang like a man working through a prayer, each hold a syllable, each dyno a breath, the whole route a conversation between his body and the thing he was trying not to think about.

"You're going to kill yourself," I said.

He didn't look down. "That's not how it works."

"It's exactly how it works. You fall from that height onto that pad and the pad does nothing and you break your back or your neck and then the newspaper writes a story about how another climber died because climbing is dangerous, except it isn't dangerous. Climbing without a rope at thirty feet when you haven't slept in a week is dangerous. There's a difference."

He paused on a jug — a big, solid hold — and hung there, one arm extended, the other resting. From below, he looked like a man crucified on the wall, arms wide, body pressed against the rock, and the image was so heavy with the symbolism he'd probably enjoy that I almost didn't say what I came to say.

Almost.

"Come down, Nate. I need to talk to you and I'm not going to talk to the bottom of your shoes."

He hung there for another five seconds. Ten. The silence in the empty gym was the loudest thing I'd heard since the night after Marcus Wells died and I stood in my own empty club and listened to the refrigerators cycle and the ice machine drop a load and the particular, haunted quiet of a room where something terrible has happened and the room hasn't processed it yet. His whole body went still, the way a climber goes still on a wall when they've run out of obvious holds and they're scanning for the next move and the next move isn't there.

Then he climbed down. Not dropped — climbed, downward, reversing each move with the technical precision of a man who is showing you that he could have done the route with his eyes closed, that the recklessness was a choice, not a failure. He stepped off the wall at the five-foot mark and landed on the crash pad and sat down on it, legs extended, chalk on his pants, sweat on his temples. He looked young. He looked like what he was — a twenty-three-year-old kid who had gotten into something so far over his head that the only place he felt in control was thirty feet up a wall with nothing between him and the ground.

"Owen used to solo that route," he said. "Tuesday evenings. After close. He'd put on music and solo the overhang circuit and I'd spot him from the ground even though he didn't need a spotter. It was our thing."

"Sounds like you miss him."

"I miss him every day." And it was real — the same crack in his voice I'd heard the first time, the grief surfacing like a fish breaking water before something pulled it back under. "He gave me everything, Jack. This job. This community. He taught me how to set routes. He taught me how to read a wall, how to see the problem before you start the moves. He was the first person who looked at me and saw —" He stopped.

"Saw what?"

"Saw someone who could do something." He picked at a piece of chalk on his pants. "My whole life, people have looked at me and seen the thing I'm not. Not in college. Not on a career track. Not making money. Not reliable. My mom. My uncle Ray. The girls I've dated. Everyone looks at me and sees the deficit. Owen looked at me and saw the thing I could do — climb, teach, move on a wall — and he built a job around it. He didn't ask about my credit score or my five-year plan. He asked if I could set a V8 that a beginner could read, and when I could, he handed me the keys to the route room."

"And then you fell in love with his wife."

The words landed in the empty gym like a dropped weight. Nate flinched — not dramatically, not theatrically, but with the micro-expression of a man who has been waiting for someone to say the thing that no one has said directly and is simultaneously relieved and terrified that the waiting is over.

"I didn't fall in love with Keira," he said. And he meant it. That was the thing. He meant it with the whole-body conviction of a true believer, with the earnest, undiluted certainty of a twenty-three-year-old who has organized his entire inner life around a framework that tells him his feelings are divine and his desires are destiny. "I *recognized* her. There's a difference. Falling in love is a choice. Recognition is — it's cellular. It's the moment your soul encounters its other half and your entire nervous system reorganizes. It's not something you decide. It's something that happens to you."

"Like a car accident."

"Like a homecoming."

"Nate." I sat down on a bench near the wall, so we were roughly at the same level — him on the crash pad, me on the bench, two men in an empty gym having the conversation that one of them had been rehearsing for eighteen months and the other had been dreading for about forty-five minutes. "I read the forums. Yours and hers. I know about the Recognition and the Runner and the Chaser and the karmic clearing. I know the vocabulary. What I need to know is whether the vocabulary is a language or a camouflage."

"I don't understand the question."

"Yes, you do. Did you know what Keira was going to do?"

His whole body went still, the way a climber goes still on a wall when they've run out of obvious holds and they're scanning for the next move and the next move isn't there.

"I knew the universe was going to clear the path," he said. Quiet. From somewhere deep in his chest, where the belief lived. "That's what the journey requires. The karmic partner has to be released before the twin flame union can manifest in the 3D. That's not — that's not me wanting Owen dead. That's the structure of the process. The literature is clear. The universe removes the obstacle when the twins are ready."

"And you were ready."

"We were in alignment. Both of us. Our frequencies were matched. The synchronicities were accelerating — we were seeing eleven-eleven everywhere, our dreams were converging, the tarot —"

"Nate." I kept my voice level. The bartender's voice. The voice I use when someone at the bar is about to say something they can't take back and needs a guardrail, not a wall. "I'm not asking about frequencies. I'm asking about a camming device. I'm asking about a number two Camalot that was placed in Owen's rack in a way that guaranteed it would fail. Someone who understands protection placement at an expert level — your level — reversed the orientation so that when Owen pulled the cam and placed it on muscle memory, it would seat wrong. It would hold on a static hang and blow on a fall. Someone engineered Owen's death using the exact knowledge that Owen taught them. I'm asking if you knew."

The silence was the loudest thing in the gym. Louder than the humming lights. Louder than the refrigerator in the back cycling on. Louder than the sound of my own heartbeat, which I could hear because the gym was that empty and the moment was that heavy.

"I —" He started. Stopped. Started again. "I set it." His voice was small. Twenty-three years old and small, the voice of a kid, not a co-author, not a divine masculine, just a kid sitting on a crash pad in a dead man's gym trying to find the line between what he believed and what he did and discovering that the line doesn't exist. "Tuesday night. After close. Keira had come in for a mobility class and she stayed after and we were talking about the clearing and I — I went to the office and I pulled his rack off the peg and I placed the cam. The number two. Upside down. Seated it in the sleeve so the lobes would pre-position. I knew Owen's reach. I knew his sequence on Coney Island. Second pitch, crux hands, number two in the flared section."

"You did it."

"I placed it. Keira —" He stopped. His hands pressed against his thighs as if he were trying to keep himself on the ground. "Keira was the one who said it had to happen. She said the universe had shown her the method. She'd been researching. She knew which cam, which route, which pitch. She'd been studying for months. I just — I executed. The literature calls it co-creation. She held the vision. I held the piece. That's how the DM and the DF work. It's not one person. It's the union."

"Nate." My voice was the bartender's voice. It had gone lower than I meant it to. "You put the cam in the rack. You handed him the rack the next morning. You signed the inspection log knowing what was in the bag. That's not co-creation. That's the hand on the trigger. That's the whole hand."

"Keira told me the universe would — would handle the consequence. She said my karma was clean because the intention was spiritual. She said —"

"The structure requires a dead man."

"The structure requires a karmic clearing."

"Those are the same thing, Nate. Those are the same thing said in two different languages and one of them is English and the other is the language you and Keira invented so you wouldn't have to hear what you were saying. You placed the cam. That's English. You rigged a man's gear to kill him. That's English. Everything else is a translation problem."

He put his face in his hands. The chalk from his fingers left white marks on his cheeks. He didn't cry. He did something worse — he sat there, face in his chalked hands, and said nothing, and the nothing was the sound of a man whose belief system is colliding with its consequences and the belief system is losing.

"I signed the log the next morning," he whispered. "Before he left. I wrote 'inspection clean' and I initialed it and I handed him the bag. He thanked me. He said, 'Trust your gear, verify your gear,' the way he always said it, and I laughed, because that's what you do when the owner of the gym makes his joke. I laughed."

"And then Keira drove him to the trailhead."

"She drove him because I texted her after I placed it. I told her the piece was set. She said she'd make sure he didn't re-pack the rack. She'd make sure he didn't do his pre-climb check twice. That's what she meant by driving. Not sixty seconds with the gear. Sixty seconds of distraction."

He sat on the crash pad with his face in his hands and his chalk on his cheeks and his whole body folded in on itself, and I stood in the gym that Owen Marsh had built with his hands and watched a twenty-three-year-old kid finish the sentence he'd spent eighteen months not finishing: *I did this*. Two words. The two words the mythology had been built to keep him from saying. The two words a prosecutor would bring to court the way a jeweler brings a loupe — small, specific, and decisive.

I left him there. Walked through the empty gym, past the routes Owen set and the holds Owen placed and the front desk where Keira narrated her transcendence. Pushed through the side door into the January night. Stood in the parking lot. Breathed.

The leased Outback with the cracked windshield was still there. Still expired. The car of a man who couldn't afford to renew his registration and couldn't afford a lawyer and couldn't afford to look directly at what he'd done, so he looked at the wall instead and called it a prayer and called it a practice and called it anything except what it was, which was complicity dressed in the language of the sacred.

I drove home. Called Navarro from the truck. Told him what Nate had said. Not everything — the long version could wait for a recorder and a lawyer and a room with a camera in the corner — but enough. The cam was placed Tuesday night, not Wednesday morning. The placement was Nate's hands. The plan was Keira's. The mythology was both of theirs, and the mythology had been a tool, and the tool had worked. Navarro listened without interrupting. At the end he said, "That's two charges, not one," and I said, "I know," and we hung up. The most dangerous lie is the one dressed in the language of truth, and Nate Calloway had spent eighteen months dressing a decision in enough sacred vocabulary to convince himself the hand on the cam wasn't his. The hand on the cam was his. Everything else was the translation problem that was going to cost him the next fifteen years.

CHAPTER 7: THE JOURNAL

Navarro got the warrant on a Thursday. He told me about it on Wednesday — not officially, not in any way that would survive a defense attorney's motion hearing, but at my bar, over a club soda, in the quiet shorthand of two men who have stopped pretending that their Wednesday evenings are casual.

"Keira's devices," he said. "Nate's too. Phones, laptops, tablets. The judge gave us everything on both of them."

"Based on?"

"Based on a dead man with a reversed cam and a head route-setter who walked into Summit Wall at 10:47 Tuesday night, alone, and walked back out at 11:12 with the owner's trad rack off the pegboard for twenty-five minutes. The security footage has Nate in the back office with the bag. We didn't have that footage two weeks ago because the DVR overwrites on a fourteen-day loop and Nate's the one who usually pulls the archive. He didn't pull it this time.

Didn't think to. And a Camalot pulled from the wall in Clear Creek has chalk residue on the outer lobes in a pattern consistent with reverse insertion — Nate's chalk, Friction Labs, a blend he special-orders and nobody else on the staff uses." He drank. "Also based on sixteen months of forum posts between the two of them describing, in detail, the spiritual necessity of removing a 'karmic obstacle' from a 'twin flame union.' Her lawyer is going to argue that metaphor isn't intent. My prosecutor is going to argue that sixteen months of metaphor and twenty-five minutes with a rack start to look a lot like planning."

The forensic report came back the following Tuesday. Navarro didn't come to the bar for this one. He called. His voice was flat — the professional flat that cops use when the evidence has confirmed the thing they suspected and the confirmation doesn't feel like victory. It feels like the evidence.

Keira's phone. The search history. Navarro read it to me the way a coroner reads a cause of death — clinical, itemized, without commentary, because the items speak for themselves:

Camming device failure modes. Searched at 1:47 a.m. on a Tuesday in November, two months before Owen died.

How does a cam fail on trad climbing. Searched at 2:03 a.m. same night.

Can a cam be placed to look correct but fail under load. Searched at 2:22 a.m.

Climbing accident investigation process. Searched at 2:41 a.m.

How long does a climbing death investigation take. Searched at 3:15 a.m.

Each search conducted between midnight and four in the morning. Each conducted on the home Wi-Fi, which meant she was in bed, in the house she shared with Owen, searching for ways to kill him while he slept one room away. Or maybe not one room away — maybe right next to her, because couples in their forties share beds even when the sharing has become a habit rather than a desire, and Keira Marsh may have been lying three feet from her husband, phone under the covers, screen brightness turned low, learning how to turn his equipment into his coffin.

Nate's phone had its own list. Not the architect's research — the engineer's. "Number two Camalot lobe orientation." "Inverted cam retention force flared crack." "Camalot rack position reverse." Eight searches over three nights in early December, each one narrower than the last, each one the work of a man who already understood the mechanics and was double-checking his math. And one more, from the afternoon of December 14: “Coney Island trad Clear Creek second pitch beta.” He’d climbed the route a dozen times. He didn’t need to look up the beta. He was looking up where the crux was, which piece of protection Owen would place at it, and how far the fall would be if that piece failed.

The YouTube history was worse. Cam failure videos — real climbing accidents, real falls, real gear popping under load. Keira had watched dozens. Not randomly, not out of curiosity — systematically, the way a student studies for an exam. She’d watched videos of cams failing in flared cracks. Cams failing when inverted. Cams failing in limestone versus granite versus sandstone. She’d watched a video titled “How Protection Fails: Common Placement Errors” four times in one week, and on the fifth viewing she’d paused it at the three-minute mark — the moment the instructor demonstrates an inverted placement — and taken a screenshot. Nate had watched the same video. From his phone. On the gym’s Wi-Fi. On a Tuesday afternoon between route-setting sessions, the way another man might watch a highlight reel between meetings.

The screenshot was in her photo gallery. Filed in an album called "Studio Marketing," between pictures of Inner Mountain's lobby and a promotional flyer for a breathwork workshop. Camouflage. The deliberate filing of murder research among innocent images, the same way she'd filed her desire for Nate among spiritual vocabulary — hidden in plain sight, dressed in the language of something harmless.

And then the texts. Navarro read them to me and I sat at my bar and listened and felt the specific nausea of a man hearing two people plan a murder without once using a word that a prosecutor could hold up in court and call a smoking gun.

Keira to Nate, November 14: *The karmic clearing is near. I can feel it in the field. The 3D obstacle is reaching its completion point. Trust the process. Trust our connection. The universe knows the timeline.*

Nate to Keira, November 14: *I feel it too. The synchronicities are accelerating. I saw 11:11 three times today. The DM/DF union is coming into alignment. I'm holding space for whatever needs to happen.*

Keira to Nate, December 3: *I've been doing research on protection — spiritual protection. How to clear karmic bonds safely. How to ensure the transition is clean and the energy doesn't attach. I want us to be ready when the clearing happens.*

Nate to Keira, December 3: *You're so thorough. That's what I love about your energy. You prepare. You don't just surrender to the flow — you co-create with it. That's the mark of an awakened DF.*

Nate to Keira, December 16, 11:08 p.m.: *It's done. The piece is set. The alignment is complete on my end. Now the universe carries it.*

Keira to Nate, December 16, 11:11 p.m.: *11:11. I received the sign the moment your message arrived. Drive tomorrow confirmed. I'll hold the field until the transition.*

Protection. She wrote "protection" and meant climbing protection — camming devices, the mechanics of failure. He wrote "the piece is set" and meant the piece was set. The vocabulary had always been a translation, and the translation broke, and underneath the breakage was a conspiracy, written in two keyboards over sixteen months of forum posts and midnight conversations, designed — the cold, architectural genius of it — to make a murder sound like metamorphosis right up until a defense attorney tries to explain to a jury why a man sent a text saying "the piece is set" the night before his boss climbed a wall holding that piece.

Never sexual. Navarro said that twice. Never explicit about the affair. Until the December 16 exchange, never a sentence that a defense attorney couldn't have reframed as spiritual dialogue between two consenting adults exploring a shared belief system. The genius of the twin flame framework — and it was genius, the cold, architectural genius of a system that can contain anything including homicide — was that it provided a vocabulary for every stage of the process. Desire became "Recognition." Obsession became "the Runner/Chaser dynamic." Planning became "co-creating with the universal flow." And murder became "karmic clearing" — a necessary event, a spiritual milestone, a box to check on the way to divine union. But even the best vocabulary breaks when a man types "the piece is set" at 11:08 on the night before his boss dies, and a prosecutor puts the text on a screen next to a photograph of the reversed Camalot, and asks the jury which one of those sentences requires translation.

The journal entries were the last thing Navarro read me. Keira kept a digital journal in a notes app, locked behind a six-digit passcode that the forensic team cracked in forty minutes. The entries spanned eighteen months and read like the diary of a woman descending — not into madness, which would be easier to prosecute and easier to forgive, but into certainty. Into the absolute, unquestioning conviction that she was doing the right thing, that the universe had given her a mission, that Owen's death was not a crime but a *correction,* a spiritual recalibration that would free both her and Nate to fulfill their divine purpose.

The last entry was written the morning of Owen's death. The morning she drove him to Clear Creek Canyon. The morning she kissed him goodbye at the tailgate and handed him a water bottle and leaned on the fender to distract him while he shouldered a rack that had been rigged thirty-six hours earlier in the back office of his own gym, by the kid he trusted with his routes and his teaching and, in the end, with the specific piece of metal that was going to kill him.

The entry was short. Three sentences. Navarro read them and I closed my eyes.

Today the clearing happens. I am in full alignment. The universe provides and I receive.

I sat at my bar after Navarro hung up. The club was closed. The Christmas lights were still blinking — the members had asked me to leave them up through

February, and I'd agreed, because arguing with Diane Kessler about decorative lighting is a battle no man wins. The lights blinked. The ice machine hummed. And I thought about the thing that turned my stomach — not the planning, not the searches, not the inverted cam or the screenshot filed under "Studio Marketing." The thing that turned my stomach was the sincerity.

She meant it. Every word. Every search, every text, every journal entry — she meant it the way a priest means a prayer, the way a soldier means a salute, the way a child means it when they tell you they saw a monster under the bed. Keira Marsh killed her husband with the full, unwavering belief that she was participating in a cosmic event, that Owen's death was a necessary condition of her spiritual evolution, that the grief she would perform at the front desk of his gym was not an act but a *stage* — a phase in the twin flame journey, documented on the forums, validated by the community, as natural and inevitable as the seasons.

And Nate. Nate meant it too. The kid on the crash pad with the chalk on his cheeks and the trembling hands and the vocabulary that made complicity sound like devotion. He meant every word about the Recognition and the

Runner and the Chaser and the karmic clearing. He meant it the way twenty-three-year-olds mean things — with the full-body commitment of a person who has never been forced to reconcile faith with consequence and who has never had enough money or status to learn that the world doesn't rearrange itself around your feelings.

Faith is a powerful thing. It's also, in the wrong hands, a weapon with no serial number — untraceable, deniable, and capable of killing a man without the killer ever feeling the recoil.

CHAPTER 8: THE BAR

Friday night. Courts full, lights on, the sound of paddles and laughter and the particular acoustic signature of my club when it's working the way it's supposed to work — the crack of polymer on polymer, the squeak of court shoes, the murmur of people keeping score, the louder murmur of people arguing about the score. The specific sound of my world. The world I built. The world I almost lost to my own entanglement with Marcus Wells's money and am now holding onto with a seven-percent credit-union loan and a cheaper pinot noir and the monthly payment that reminds me, on the fifteenth of every month, that I am not above the consequences of my own bad judgment.

Sandra — my Thursday-through-Saturday server, the one who remembers every member's name and tolerates none of their nonsense — was moving between tables with the efficient grace of a woman who has been doing this work long enough to make it look easy and short enough time to still care about doing it well. I was behind the bar, doing the thing I do, which is pour drinks and watch people and pretend that the watching is incidental to the pouring when in fact the pouring is incidental to the watching. It's always been this way. The bar is the cover. The eyes are the job.

Navarro came in at nine-fifteen. He didn't sit at his usual stool — the far end, closest to the wall. He sat at the near end, closest to the door, which meant he wasn't staying long or he had something to say that he wanted to say quickly. I poured his Topo Chico without asking. Set it on a napkin. He picked it up immediately, which was unusual — normally he lets it sit, lets the condensation build, turns the glass in his hands the way a man handles a thing he's thinking about. Tonight he drank. Set it down.

"She's not going to plead guilty," he said.

I leaned against the back counter. Crossed my arms. Waited.

"Her attorney filed the initial response today. Not guilty. She's going to trial." He looked at the club soda. "She doesn't think she did anything wrong, Jack. I've interviewed her three times now. Three sessions, four hours each. And every time — every single time — she tells me the same thing, in the same calm, centered voice, with the same vocabulary she uses on the forums and in her journal and in those midnight texts. She says Owen's death was 'a karmic clearing.' She says the universe 'chose the timeline.' She says her role was to 'align her intention with the universal flow' and that what happened on the wall was not murder but 'a transition facilitated by divine timing.'"

"She thinks she's innocent."

"She *knows* she's innocent. That's the part that keeps me up. She's not performing innocence — I've seen that, I know what it looks like, people who've done the thing and are running the calculations on how to avoid the consequence. Keira's not calculating. She's *serene*. She genuinely believes that the universe killed Owen and she just — assisted. That she was a vessel. An instrument. That her research and her planning and the message she sent Nate to set the piece were all part of a process that was bigger than her, and that questioning the process would be like questioning gravity. She says she never touched the rack. And that's true, by the way. Forensically, she never touched it. She didn't have to."

"The jury's going to love that."

"The jury's going to hear an expert witness on cult psychology explain how closed ideological systems create moral frameworks that override conventional ethics. The prosecution is bringing in a professor from CU Boulder who specializes in high-demand groups. The defense is bringing in a spiritual advisor who's going to testify that twin flame belief is a 'legitimate metaphysical framework' and that Keira's actions were 'consistent with the internal logic of her faith tradition.'"

"Her faith tradition told her to kill her husband."

"Her faith tradition told her to align with the universal timeline. The gap between those two sentences is where the trial is going to happen."

"And Nate?"

"Nate's cooperating. Public defender — kid doesn't have two thousand dollars for a retainer, let alone a real defense." Navarro turned the glass again. The old motion, the thinking motion. "His lawyer is building the vessel defense. Same one Keira is using, but inverted. Keira says the universe moved through her planning. Nate's going to say the universe moved through his hands. That Keira told him the alignment required a physical component and he performed the component without understanding it as an act of violence, because inside the belief system he and Keira had built together there was no such thing as violence, there was only the universe expressing itself through willing instruments. That when he wrote 'the piece is set' at eleven-oh-eight on a Tuesday night, he meant a spiritual alignment and not a number two Camalot. That he believed the mythology so completely he couldn't see the method even when his own hands were performing it."

"Do you buy that?"

Navarro was quiet for a long time. Long enough that Sandra came by and refilled his water glass — regular water, the backup — and he thanked her with the absent politeness of a man whose attention is somewhere else. The club noise washed around us. Paddles. Laughter. The sound of a community doing the thing communities do, which is exist in proximity and call it connection.

"I don't buy it," Navarro said finally. "And the D.A. doesn't either. The D.A. has spent the last two weeks reading Colorado Revised Statutes out loud to anyone who'll listen. Section 18-1-603. Complicity. A person is legally accountable for the behavior of another if, with the intent to promote or facilitate the commission of the offense, he aids, abets, advises, or encourages the other person in planning or committing the offense. Read that sentence and then look at what Nate actually did. He researched the retention properties of an inverted number two Camalot in a flared crack. He watched the same YouTube video Keira watched, on the same night, from his own phone. He placed the cam in Owen's rack on a Tuesday night at ten forty-seven p.m., on camera, alone in the back office, for twenty-five minutes. He signed the inspection log the next morning certifying that Owen's gear was sound. He texted Keira 'the piece is set, the alignment is complete on my end' at eleven-oh-eight that night. He coordinated the Friday drive with her knowing what was in the rack on the passenger seat. That's not a bystander. That's not a man who chose not to know. That's every single element of complicity to murder in the first degree, laid out in order, with time stamps."

"Complicity carries the same sentence as the principal offense," I said. I wasn't asking.

"Same statute, same penalty. In Colorado, first-degree murder after deliberation is a Class 1 felony. Life without parole. If complicity sticks — and the D.A. thinks it will, because the texts and the search history and the video and the signed inspection log all line up in a way juries tend to find persuasive — Nate eats the same sentence Keira does. The accessory charge is a separate count, a Class 4 felony under 18-8-105 for rendering assistance after the fact — the fresh-chalk inspection sign-off, the texts the next morning, the drive coordination. That's belt and suspenders. The main thing is the complicity."

"So they're both looking at life."

"They're both looking at life. Keira because she planned it. Nate because he performed it. The D.A.'s office calls it a two-hand murder. One hand did the thinking, one hand did the placing, and the law in this state doesn't care which hand is which — it cares that they were attached to the same intent, and the texts prove they were."

"And Nate's lawyer still thinks the vessel defense has legs."

"Nate's lawyer is a public defender with a hundred and forty active cases and a client who confessed on video, who kept the Camalot's box in his closet with the original packaging, who Googled 'Clear Creek second pitch beta' from his own phone the week before the fall. Nate's lawyer is going to plead him down to second-degree or manslaughter if she can and call it a career. The vessel defense is what Nate tells himself in his cell at night. It's not what's going in a filing." Navarro drank off the last of the Topo Chico. "He's twenty-three years old. He's going to be sixty before he's out, if he's out at all. And he's going to spend every one of those years trying to figure out whether believing something hard enough makes you responsible for the thing you believed in. The law already answered that question. He just hasn't heard the answer yet."

I wiped the bar. The automatic motion. The thing my hands do when my brain is somewhere else, the muscle memory of a man who has been polishing this same stretch of mahogany for twelve years and has cleaned up more messes than the ones you can see.

I thought about the distance between Vanessa Kline and Keira Marsh. Two women who removed the man between them and the life they wanted. Vanessa knew what she was doing and called it justice. She looked at Marcus Wells with the clear eyes of a woman who had made a calculation and was willing to pay the price. There was something almost honest in that — the honesty of a person who has dropped the pretense and is operating in the open, even if the operation is murder. Keira was the opposite. Keira had wrapped the murder in so many layers of spiritual meaning that the murder itself had disappeared, the way a gift disappears inside wrapping paper and the person opening it has forgotten that the paper isn't the point. And then there was Nate, who was neither — not Vanessa's clear-eyed calculator and not Keira's serene architect. Nate was the hand. The hand that did the thing the planner wouldn't touch. The hand that believed the paper was the point and was now going to spend the rest of his life in a room where the law cared only about what the hand had done.

All three of them are going to spend the rest of their lives in a room where the walls don't care what you call it.

Navarro finished his drink. Set the glass on the bar. Placed a ten next to it, the way he always does — overpaying for a club soda because the overpayment is how he says thank you without saying thank you, and I accept the overpayment because accepting it is how I say you're welcome without the conversation that neither of us wants to have about what, exactly, the other is providing.

He stood up. Pulled on his jacket.

"Same time next month?"

"You buying?"

"I'm buying."

He walked to the door. Stopped. Turned back.

"The title," he said. "Of Owen's blog post about gear inspection. 'Trust Your Gear, Verify Your Gear.' I keep thinking about that. He wrote the rule. He taught the rule. He lived the rule with everyone's gear except the gear that killed him, because the gear that killed him had passed through two sets of hands he didn't verify — the wife who loved him and the kid he trained — and Owen Marsh trusted both of them the way he trusted his gear, completely, automatically, without verification, because verifying the people you love feels like an accusation, and Owen Marsh was not a man who accused."

He left.

I locked up. Turned off the court lights. Checked the patio doors. Set the alarm. Walked through the club one last time, the way I always do — the rooms emptying, the shadows settling, the building exhaling into the silence of a place that exists to hold noise and is now holding the absence of it.

The Christmas lights were still on. Blinking in the January dark. Diane Kessler's lights. The lights that the members asked me to keep because the club looked better with them, softer, warmer, less like a place where a man was murdered and more like a place where people come to play a game and drink a drink and pretend, for an hour or two, that the world outside the glass is someone else's problem.

I stood behind the bar in the quiet. My bar. The bar I built and nearly lost and rebuilt with borrowed money and cheaper wine and the stubborn refusal to close that is either my greatest strength or my most expensive flaw, and I have stopped trying to figure out which because the answer doesn't change the payment.

I picked up a cloth. Started wiping down the mahogany. The motion was the same as it always is — circular, slow, thorough, the motion of a man cleaning up after the day's messes, the seen ones and the unseen ones, the spilled drinks and the spilled lives. Twelve years of this. Twelve years of watching. Twelve years of reading rooms and pouring drinks and standing behind a counter while people sit on the other side of it and tell me things they don't tell anyone else, because the bartender is the last secular priest and the bar is the last confessional and the drinks are the sacrament and none of it saves anyone but all of it helps, a little, in the specific and limited way that being heard helps — not because the hearing fixes the problem but because the hearing makes the problem bearable, and bearable, in my experience, is the most that most people can hope for.

I noticed that one of the strings of lights just went out. One more thing to work on.

www.ingramcontent.com/pod-product-compliance
Lightning Source LLC
LaVergne TN
LVHW010630100826
845148LV00014B/3182
9798950176005